HERE A GHOST,
THERE A GHOST

HERE A GHOST

THERE A GHOST

by Elizabeth P. Hoffman

illustrated by David Kingham

Julian Messner New York

Published by Julian Messner, a Simon & Schuster
Division of Gulf & Western Corporation, Simon &
Schuster Building, 1230 Avenue of the Americas,
New York, N.Y. 10020.

Manufactured in the United States of America

Design by David Kingham

Second Printing, 1979

Library of Congress Cataloging in Publication Data
Hoffman, Elizabeth, 1921–
Here a ghost, there a ghost.

Includes index.
1. Ghosts—Juvenile literature. I. Kingham, David.
II. Title.
BF1461.H58 133.1 78-2544
ISBN 0-671-32851-4

CONTENTS

Chapter
One Ghosts—What Are They? 7
Two Investigators of Ghosts 15
Three New Ghosts 27
Four Old Ghosts 34
Five Noisy Ghosts 44
Six Ghosts of Living People 56
Seven Other Kinds of Ghosts 63
Eight Pictures of Ghosts 71
Nine Real Ghosts and Imaginary Ghosts 81
Glossary 87
Some Legendary Ghosts and Haunted Houses in the United States 89
Index 94

To my husband, Huff,
who has been with me
on many ghostly adventures

GHOSTS —WHAT ARE THEY?

CHAPTER ONE

Are there really such things as ghosts? Many people believe in them. This belief is more than just saying that an old house is "haunted." It's more than being superstitious about walking in cemeteries after dark, or looking into cracked mirrors.

It is believed by many that all people have a *spirit.* The spirit is the part of a person that remembers its experiences, and lives. It is also called "life" or "life force." It is the spirit that makes a person different from every other person. Some people believe that the spirit of a dead person or animal can make itself known to the living, even though its body has died.

the railroad track. Then comes the sound of an approaching train. Finally, a deafening crash.

The real accident happened when a train developed engine trouble and stalled on the track. Someone from that train must have run desperately back toward the speeding approaching train, swinging the lantern as a signal. But the warning either came too late, or went unnoticed.

The entire area where this ghost accident is repeated over and over again has been examined. There is nothing that could make such a tremendous crash.

The Borley Rectory in England, along with its other spirits, was visited by the ghosts of a coach and team of horses.

Edward Cooper and his wife lived in a small cottage near the Rectory in 1916. On a moonlight night, something made him look out the window. He saw lights moving across the field. As they came closer, he discovered that they were lamps on an old coach. Two coachmen sat on the high front seat and drove a pair of horses. The coach moved straight through the hedge as though it weren't there, and into the Rectory yard. Then it disappeared.

Before the Rectory burned, other people told about seeing the coach. Others could not see it, but clearly heard the unmistakable sounds of running horses and racing coach wheels.

PICTURES OF GHOSTS

CHAPTER EIGHT

If a thing exists, some people say, you can take a picture of it or make a recording of it. That is not quite true. Try photographing or recording the smell of a rose. But if it *were* true, pictures alone could prove the existence of ghosts.

Two well-known photographs of ghosts were made in England. While visiting the Naval College in Greenwich, London, in the 1960's, the Reverend Ralph Hardy and his wife decided to take a picture of the famous Tulip Staircase. When the Hardys' film was developed and printed, a robed figure could be seen going up the steps.

The Tulip Staircase. (Courtesy of Rev. Hardy) ►

Part of a second figure was also present, and some who have studied the print believe they see the arm of a third person. Mr. Hardy took the picture from one side of the staircase. Mrs. Hardy was beside him. No one else was there.

Experts who examined the film agreed that no one had tampered with it. The Hardys had photographed a ghost, maybe even two or three.

The Naval College had formerly been a palace. Henry the Eighth was born there, as were his daughters Queen Mary and Queen Elizabeth the First. Henry was married several times there, and his son, Edward the Seventh, died there. Later, the palace became a naval hospital. Events in the lives of many people seem to have resulted in many ghosts. So it's impossible to know whom the Hardys photographed.

The other well-known picture of a ghost was taken by accident in 1936 in Raynham Hall, as reported by the British Psychic Society. For many years, the Hall had been haunted by the "Brown Lady." Some people who saw her thought she looked like a member of the family who had lived there two hundred years earlier. There was a portrait of the lady wearing a brown dress hanging in the Hall.

Two professional photographers, Captain Provand and Indse Shiea, were taking pictures inside the house, including some shots of the main oak staircase. Shiea saw something moving down the stairs that looked like a veiled figure. He could also see the steps through the figure, because the figure was like a thin cloud, although it had the shape of a person. Shiea called to Captain Provand, whose head was under the camera cloth, to take the picture.

When the negative was developed, there was a hazy, cloudy figure coming down the steps. Many people who didn't believe in ghosts tried to prove the picture was a trick, but no one ever succeeded. The photographers had asked a man to come to their shop to look at the film while it was in the developing solution that is used in making pictures show on film. He could testify that the finished picture was just what had been recorded on the film when the shot was taken.

To make pictures like these, something must exist that can make an impression or imprint on film. Some people say it is a trick of light. But they have not studied carefully the events going on as the picture was being taken. Where does the ghost image that is being photographed come from? No one is really sure.

Some investigators who study pictures of ghosts feel that if the ghost loved a person or a place very deeply, they may be photographed together. The "Brown Lady" must have lived in Raynham Hall and loved it very much.

The love held by a ghost for a living person may have something to do with a picture unexpectedly taken in Norristown, Pennsylvania. A girl in a high school photography class was learning how to load a camera with film, take a picture, remove the film, develop it, and finally make a print.

When she herself was photographed by a member of the class, she was astonished to find behind her in the finished picture, the image of her aunt, who had died six years earlier. The girl's mother also recognized her sister.

When the mother and daughter searched for an explanation, they could find none. The photograph had been taken in the school, not in the girl's home where a picture of her aunt might have been in the background of the area recorded on the film.

When a psychic investigated, she learned that the girl had been cared for by her aunt for several years when her mother had been ill. The investigator believed that because they had such a close relationship for all that time, the aunt's ghost must have been actually present when the picture was taken.

Since ghosts have been photographed in still pictures, some people have reasoned that movies

◀ *The "Brown Lady" of Raynham Hall. (Photograph from the files of Fate Magazine)*

could be taken of them. In a home in England, a ball of light was seen and filmed while moving out of one door and disappearing behind another. Was the moving object ball lightning as some people believed?

Lightning does sometimes appear in balls instead of jagged lines. But ball lightning, like the jagged kind, appears only during thunderstorms. When the rolling ball of light was photographed by a motion picture camera, there was no storm.

Hans Holzer, the parapsychologist, has photographed ghosts of monks walking down the aisle of a cathedral. They seemed to be very short men. But an investigation showed that the floor in the cathedral had been raised. The old floor was several inches lower than the new one. The ghosts would have been as tall as average adults if they had been walking on the new floor.

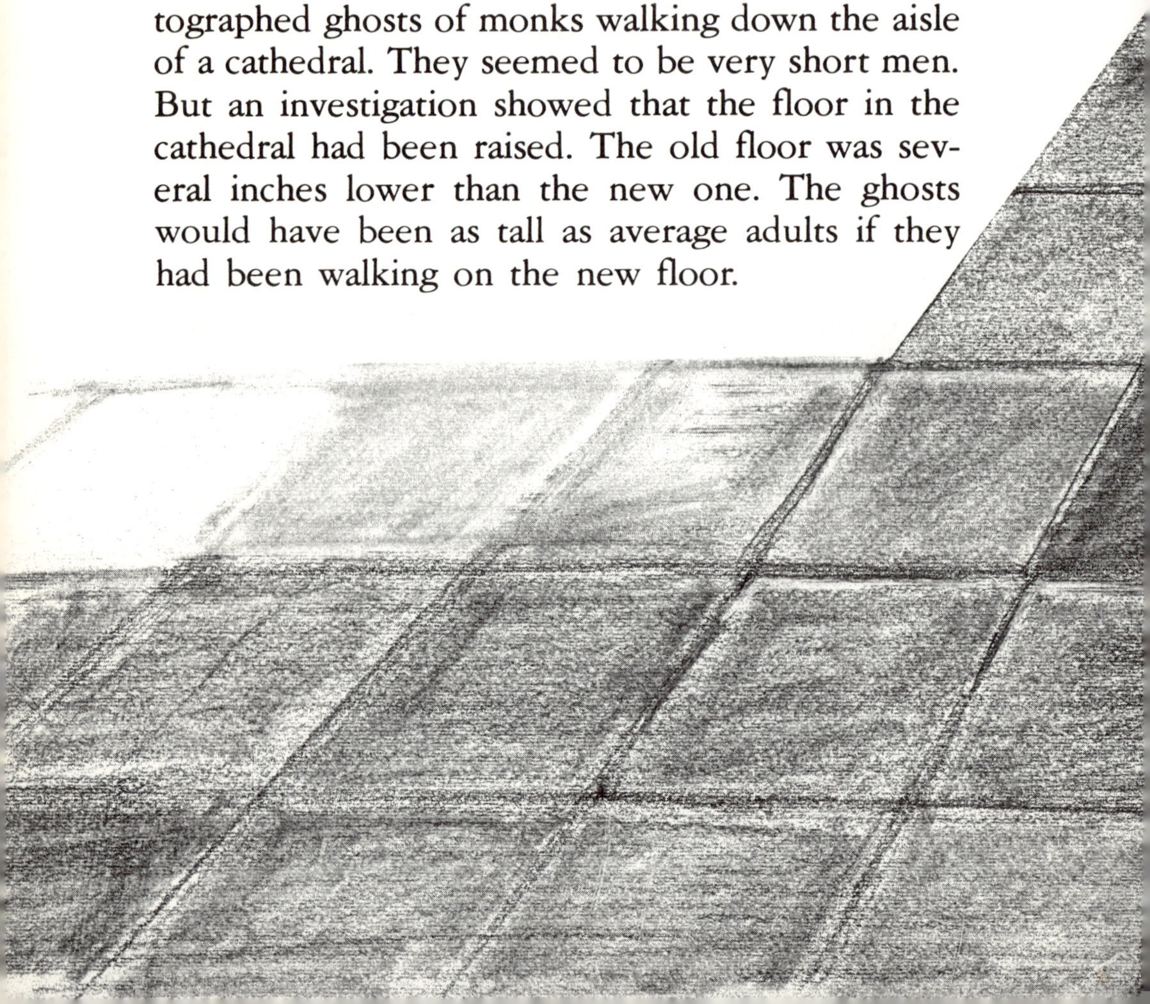

Investigators cannot be sure they will take a picture of a ghost if they go searching for one with a camera. Ghosts seem to appear when you least expect them. This may be because only a piece of the ghost's story is known. We don't know why the ghosts seemed to be walking up the Tulip Staircase, or down the steps in Raynham Hall, or why the girl's aunt apparently was in the high school room. Other investigators may someday answer these questions.

REAL GHOSTS AND IMAGINARY GHOSTS

CHAPTER NINE

When you read a story like Georgie the Ghost or The Marshmallow Ghost, or watch a TV show like Casper the Friendly Ghost, you know they are pretend or imaginary ghosts. Their stories have a beginning, a middle, and an end. As the story goes along, you find out about the ghost and other characters. They become involved in one or more problems. At the end of the story, all of the pieces are brought together for a happy ending.

But a real experience a person has with a ghost is only part of a story. Sometimes we know who or what the ghost is, and sometimes we don't. If the ghost tries to communicate, we may understand it, or it may fail to make its message clear to us.

The real life experience of seeing, or hearing, or sensing a ghost is like watching a television show for a few minutes in the middle of the story. You don't know how the story started, what happened until the few minutes you saw, or how it ended. That is why many accounts of real ghosts don't make much sense by themselves.

Ralph Harlow was a minister and a professor of history at Smith College. He was very much interested in psychic phenomena. He talked with people who had experiences of this type and performed some experiments. He believed the spirits of people live after death.

One day a biology professor told Dr. Harlow that he would not believe in psychic experiences until he could choose the exact place and the manner in which they would happen. Dr. Harlow then told his friend that if he could make butterflies come out of a cocoon on a December day, at noon, on the wall of the Science Building, then he, Dr. Harlow, would believe that butterflies are held in cocoons. Naturally his friend couldn't promise that. As you read about ghosts, remember proof of their existence is almost impossible to find.

And because proof is so hard to find, there are many people who try to fool others by tricks and magic. Sometimes it is very hard to discover these tricks, and clearly separate them from real ghost experiences.

There are some mediums who only pretend to see or hear or talk to ghosts. Others are honestly misled by things that happen in nature, which they do not understand very well or not at all. Sometimes a trick of light or a movement of the wind makes people think that they have seen a ghost, when they really haven't.

When you read about ghosts or hear ghost stories, think about the details of such reports, and ask questions before you accept all of the story as true. Imaginary ghost stories are lots of fun. Stories of ghosts that seem to be real are fun, too.

Investigators have shown that the same happening or sight will be described differently by everyone who saw or experienced it. This is what makes it hard to tell what *really* happened. Errors are so easy to make, but so hard to find out and correct.

The best way to study about ghosts is to learn all you can from several different reports of the same ghost experience. Then keep eyes and ears open and report anything you see as honestly and as carefully as you can. It is a great thrill to have experienced a ghost, for very few people get a chance to do so. And many people who have had the experience are sometimes unwilling to tell about it, for fear that others will laugh at them. But if you are honest and careful about your observations and are at the right place at the right time, you can have the last laugh. It can happen to anyone.

GLOSSARY

Conscious—The part of the mind that is awake and knows, and controls everyday life. *See also* Subconscious.

Dream—A series of pictures or happenings seen while a person is sleeping.

Experience—An event or happening.

Ghost—The spirit of a person, animal or thing known to be dead, but seen by the living and therefore seeming to be alive.

Haunting—The experiencing of a ghost many times in the same place, usually a house or building.

Investigator—A person who searches and gathers information.

Medium—A person who can gather information while seeming to be alseep, and giving it to a person who is awake. *See also* Subconscious.

Parapsychologist—A person who investigates ghosts and/or any other unusual event or happening.

Poltergeist—A ghost that is always invisible, but makes itself known by throwing things, moving furniture, or making a loud noise.

Psychic—A person who learns information by sensing or feeling, rather than by seeing or studying.

Psychokinesis—"Mind movement," that is, the moving of any object using only the mind as the force.

Psychologist—A person who studies the human mind, and helps other people in their thinking.

Spirit—That part of a person that remembers experiences and feelings. It is alive, and is also called "life" or "life force."

Subconscious—The part of the mind that takes over in sleep or in dreams, or when a person goes into a trance. *See* Trance.

Superstition—A belief or an idea that does not come from facts.

Telepathy—Sending thoughts to a person without using any of the senses—that is, without sound, sight, touch or smell.

Trance—A kind of sleep in which the conscious part of the mind is asleep, but the subconscious part of the mind is awake, and can contact spirits.

SOME LEGENDARY GHOSTS AND HAUNTED HOUSES IN THE UNITED STATES

ATTRACTION	FEATURES	CONTACT	SEASONS AND HOURS
Beauregard House (LeCarpentier House) New Orleans, Louisiana	This handsome columned residence was rented to Civil War General P.G.T. Beauregard, who is said to still haunt the building.	Beauregard House 1113 Chartres Street New Orleans, Louisiana 70116 Tel. (504) 523-7257	Monday-Saturday 10:00 a.m.-4:00 p.m. (Admission)
Belle Grove Middletown, Virginia	Belle Grove is a beautiful plantation house set in the Shenandoah Mountains. Restored as a museum, its historic past includes a bizarre murder and tales of ghosts around the smoke house.	Belle Grove Box 137 Middletown, Va. 22645 Tel. (703) 869-2028	April-October 10:00 a.m.-4:00 p.m. Sunday 1:00 p.m.-5:00 p.m. (Admission)
The Cottage Plantation (ruins) Baton Rouge, Louisiana	This haunted plantation, now in ruins, was once a magnificent columned estate visited by Marquis de Lafayette and many American notables.	The Cottage Plantation Route 5 Box 425 St. Francisville, Louisiana 70775 Tel. (504) 635-3674	Open year round.
Decatur House Washington, D.C.	This house, situated across Lafayette Park from The White House, is haunted by the spirit of its first owner, Stephen Decatur, a naval hero who died in a tragic duel.	National Trust for Historic Preservation 748 Jackson Place, N.W. Washington, D.C. 20006 Tel. (202) 638-5200	Monday-Friday 10:00 a.m.-2:00 p.m. Saturday, Sunday & Holidays Noon-4:00 p.m.
Fort Monroe Hampton, Virginia (near Norfolk)	Fort Monroe is the oldest continually garrisoned fortress in the USA, housing at least 10 spirits in its private residences and military casements.	Fort Monroe Casemate Museum Box 341 Fort Monroe Fort Monroe, Virginia 23651 Tel. (804) 727-3935 or 3391	Weekdays 8:00 a.m.-5:00 p.m. Weekends 10:30 a.m.-5:00 p.m.
Haw Branch Plantation Amelia County, Virginia	This private residence, built in 1745, is a fine example of Georgian-Federal architecture and a happy haunting ground for a myriad of ghosts.	Mr. W.C. McConnaughey Box 188 Amelia, Virginia 23002 Tel. (804) 561-2472	Daily 10:00 a.m.-5:00 p.m. (Admission)

ATTRACTION	FEATURES	CONTACT	SEASONS AND HOURS
Kenmore Fredericksburg, Virginia	Kenmore, a gracious home of Georgian design, is said to be haunted by Colonel Fielding Lewis, a Revolutionary patriot who organized the Virginia Militia and made armaments for the rebels.	Kenmore Association 1201 Washington Avenue Fredericksburg, Virginia 22401 Tel. (703) 373-3381 or 2363	March-November 9:00 a.m.-5:00 p.m. Winter 9:00 a.m.-4:00 p.m. (Admission)
Lee's Boyhood Home Alexandria, Virginia	This beautifully furnished home was once owned by "Light Horse" Harry Lee, a Revolutionary War hero and father of General Robert E. Lee. The home is haunted by a little boy who many agree is the ghost of Robert E. Lee himself.	Robert E. Lee House 607 Oronoco Street Alexandria, Virginia 22314 Tel. (202) 548-8454	Open daily with guided tours from 10 a.m. to 4 p.m. Closed December 15-February 1. (Admission)
Loudoun Mansion Germantown, Pennsylvania	This restored home of a prominent 19th century merchant is filled with 18th century antiques and haunted by the spirit of a small boy.	Loudoun Mansion 4650 Germantown Avenue Germantown, Pennsylvania 19144 Tel. (215) 843-3388	Open from 1:00 p.m. to 4:00 p.m. on Tuesdays and Thursdays and the first and third Sunday of each month. (Admission)
Marine Antique Shop Wiscassett, Maine	The Marine Antique Shop was once a restaurant where employees reported seeing chairs and tables moving.	Wiscassett Chamber of Commerce P.O. Box 274 Wiscassett, Maine 04578 Tel. (207) 882-7208	Monday-Saturday 9:00 a.m.-5:00 p.m.
Musical Wonder House Wiscassett, Maine	Spirits chatter at the Musical Wonder House, a museum containing over 250 mechanical music machines.	Wiscassett Chamber of Commerce P.O. Box 274 Wiscassett, Maine 04578 Tel. (207) 882-7163	June 1-Labor Day Monday-Friday 10:00 a.m.-5:00 p.m. Sunday 1:00 p.m.-5:00 p.m. September and October Weekends 10:00 a.m.-5:00 p.m.
Oaklawn Manor Franklin, Louisiana	This white-pillared mansion with marble floors contains fine European antiques. Henry Clay visited here often and today returns in spirit form.	Oaklawn Manor Franklin, Louisiana 70538 Phone: (318) 828-0236	Daily 8:30 a.m.-4:30 p.m. (Admission)

The Octagon Washington, D.C.	Built by one of the wealthiest men in the U.S. during the 1700's, the Octagon House is steeped in legend and tales of ghosts.	The Octagon 1799 New York Avenue, N.W. Washington, D.C. 20006 Tel. (202) 638-3105	Tuesday-Saturday 10:00 a.m.-4:00 p.m. Sunday 1:00 p.m.-4:00 p.m.
Parlange Plantation New Roads, Louisiana	Parlange, a classic example of raised construction popular with the early Louisiana settlers, is haunted by the spirit of a lovely young girl.	Parlange Plantation Route 1 Box M73A New Roads, Louisiana 70760 Tel. (504) 638-8410	Daily 9:00 a.m.-5:00 p.m. (Admission)
Ramsay House Alexandria, Virginia	The Ramsay House, now the site of Alexandria's Visitors Center, was once the home of William Ramsay, a Scottish merchant, city founder and first Lord Mayor. Reputedly the spirit of Ramsay appears on occcasion at an upstairs window.	Alexandria Tourist Council 221 King Street Alexandria, Virginia 22314 Tel. (202) 549-0205	Daily 10:00 a.m.-5:00 p.m.
St. Louis Cemetery Number 1 New Orleans, Louisiana	This old city cemetery is full of above-ground tombs, a method of burial that the damp Louisiana earth demands. Those who believe that the Voodoo Queen, Marie Levaux is buried here mark her tomb with hex signs and knock three times to have their wishes answered.	Greater New Orleans Tourist & Convention Commission 334 Royal Street New Orleans, Louisiana 70130 Tel. (504) 522-8772	Open to public in daylight hours.
St. Maurice Plantation St. Maurice, Louisiana	Tales persist that this massive home is haunted by a child who rises from the cemetery and by spirits who noisily turn calendar pages.	St. Maurice Plantation St. Maurice, Louisiana 71471 Phone: (318) 646-2695	Tuesday-Saturday 9:00 a.m.-5:00 p.m. Sunday Noon-5:00 p.m. (Admission)
Scotchtown Hanover County, Virginia	One of Virginia's oldest homes, this was the home of both Patriot Patrick Henry and Dolly Madison, wife of the 4th President of the U.S. It is cloaked in legend, including one of a duel in the hall leaving bloodstains and apparitions.	Scotchtown Route 2, Box 168 Beaverdam, Virginia 23015 Tel. (804) 227-3500	April-October 10:00 a.m.-4:30 p.m. (Admission)
Shirley Plantation Charles City County, Virginia	This is the ancestral home of the King Carter family, crammed with antiques and architechtural treasures. The portrait of "Aunt Pratt" makes ghostly noises when hung wrong.	Shirley Plantation Route 2 Box 57 Charles City, Virginia 23030 Tel. (804) 795-2385	Daily 9:00 a.m.-5:00 p.m.

ATTRACTION	FEATURES	CONTACT	SEASONS AND HOURS
USF Constellation Baltimore, Maryland	Aboard this floating museum lurks the ghost of a sailor who died in 1799 and returns to clear his name of charges of cowardice.	USF Constellation Pier 1, Constellation Dock Baltimore, Maryland 21202 Tel. (301) 539-1797	Monday-Saturday 10:00 a.m.-3:45 p.m. Sunday Noon-5:45 p.m. (Admission)
Valcour Aime Plantation Gardens (ruins) Vacherie, Louisiana	Valcour Aime Plantation, once called the "Versailles of Louisiana," was the home of a wealthy planter. An unidentified spirit, perhaps the soul of Valcour Aime, haunts the grounds.	Louisiana State Tourist Division P.O. Box 44291 Baton Rouge, Louisiana 70804 Tel. (504) 389-5233	Open year round.
Westover Plantation Charles City County, Virginia (Southeast of Richmond)	This house, an outstanding example of Georgian architecture in America, is home to the ghost of Evelyn Byrd, who died of a broken heart when her father thwarted her marriage to a British nobleman.	Virginia State Travel Service 6 North Sixth Street Richmond, Virginia 23219 Tel. (804) 786-4484	Gardens open daily year round. Home can be visited during Garden Week in the Spring.
Whaley House San Diego, California	The Whaley House, San Diego's first brick mansion (1856), was also the seat of San Diego Government and courthouse during the 1860s—70s. Built by Judge Thomas Whaley on the old city executive grounds, the Whaley House is said to be haunted by an unfortunate gallows victim.	Whaley House Old Town 2482 San Diego Avenue San Diego, California 92110 Tel. (714) 298-2482	Wednesday-Sunday 10:00 a.m.-4:30 p.m. (Admission)
Winchester Mystery House San Jose, California	The Winchester Mystery House is a sprawling 160 room house that its owner expanded continuously for 35 years, feeling that if she kept building rooms for good spirits they would keep the evil ones away.	The Winchester House 525 S. Winchester Boulevard San Jose, California 95128 Phone: (408) 247-2000	Daily 9:00 a.m.-4:30 p.m. (Admission)
Woodburn (Governor's Mansion) Dover, Delaware	This is the home of Delaware's Chief Executive and also the residence of a wine-sipping ghost who empties decanters in the dining room.	Travel Development Bureau Department of Economic Development 630 State College Road Dover, Delaware 19901 Phone: (302) 678-4254	Thursday 2:00 p.m.-4:00 p.m.

Wyth House Williamsburg, Virginia	Restored home is part of the Colonial Williamsburg restoration of 160 buildings set on 173 acres. Lady Skipwith returns in 18th century ball gown to haunt this old home.	Director of Travel Colonial Williamsburg Foundation Williamsburg, Virginia 23185 Phone: (804) 229-1000	July-August 9:00 a.m.-7:00 p.m. Remainder of the year 9:00 a.m.-5:00 p.m. (Admission)
Pharmacie Francaise New Orleans, Louisiana	This museum, run by the Historical Pharmacy Commission, shows ancient cures and methods including a collection of Voodoo potions and hexes.	The Historical Pharmacy Museum 514 Chartres Street New Orleans, Louisiana 70130 Phone: (504) 586-4392	Tuesday-Saturday 10:00 a.m.-5:00 p.m.
The Voodoo Museum New Orleans, Louisiana	This museum depicts the ancient history of Voodoo and its growth in New Orleans.	The Voodoo Museum 739 Bourbon Street New Orleans, Louisiana 70116 Phone: (504) 523-2906	Daily 10:00 a.m.-11:00 p.m. (Admission)
The Myrtles Plantation St. Francisville, Louisiana	The Myrtles, the largest and oldest plantation in the State, is haunted by a French governess who appears to peer into sleeping faces in the bedroom.	The Myrtles Plantation P.O. Box 757 St. Francisville, Louisiana 70775 Attn: Steve Saunders Tel. (504) 635-6277	Daily 9:00 a.m.-5:00 p.m. Evening-by appointment (Admission)

INDEX

A
Alexandria, Virginia, 35
American Society for Psychic Research, 46
America's Most Haunted Places, 67
Amherst, Nova Scotia, 50. *See also* Great Amherst Mystery
astral projection, 61

B
Baltimore, Maryland, 37
Betty Ruth, 51
boats, 9, 67. *See also* ships
Boleyn, Anne, 37
Borley Rectory, 55, 70
Brandywine, 67
British Psychic Society, 74
Brown Lady, 74, 75
Bucks County, Pennsylvania, 39

C
Campbell, Mrs. 57, 58
cats, 13, 65, 66
conscious (mind), 20
crying. *See* sound

D
Division of Parapsychology, University of Virginia, Virginia, 46
dogs, 13
Dublin, Ireland, 23
Duke University, 46

E
Edward the Seventh, 74
Esther (Teed), 50, 51
experience, 16, 17

G
Gallery of Ghosts, 57
Godfrey, Arthur, 28, 30
Great Amherst Mystery, 50
Greene, Timothy, 42

H
Hampton Court Palace, 38
Hardy, Reverend Ralph, 72, 74

Harlow, Ralph, 84
haunting, 12, 55, 58
Henry the Eighth, 74
Hollows, The, 22
Holzer, Hans, 23, 24, 78
horses, 38, 64, 67, 70
Howard, Katherine, 38
Hudson River Valley, 67

L
Lee, Robert E., 36
Leek, Sybil, 23, 24
Lincoln, Abraham, 35, 36
Lively Ghosts of Ireland, The, 23

M
Mackenzie, Andrew, 57
Maine, 37
Mark, 59, 60
Masters, Mary, 24
medium, 20, 22, 26, 38

N
nab, 67
Naval College, Greenwich, London, 72, 74
New Hope, Pennsylvania, 39
New York, New York, 42
noise. *See* sound
Norristown, Pennsylvania, 77
North Carolina, 67

O
odor. *See* smells
out-of-the-body experience, 61. *See also* astral projection

P
parapsychologists, 16, 20, 22, 26, 33, 61
parapsychology, 16
Parapsychology Laboratory at Duke University, North Carolina, 46
Pickett, Joseph, 39, 40, 41
PK. *See* psychokinesis
poltergeists, 12, 45, 46, 50, 54, 55
Price, Harry, 55

Provand, Captain, 74, 75
psychics, 24, 25, 26
psychokinesis, 46, 51, 54

Q
Queen Elizabeth the First, 74
Queen Mary, 74

R
Raynham Hall, 74, 75, 80
Rectory. *See* Borley Rectory
Roberts, Bruce and Mary, 67
Roll, William G., 54
Rosemont, Pennsylvania, 38

S
San Jose, California, 37
Shiea, Indse, 74, 75
ships, 13, 28. *See also* boats
smells, 9, 41, 42, 43
Smith College, Massachusetts, 84
sound, 13, 17, 24, 31, 32, 41, 55
St. Louis, Missouri, 59
subconscious (mind), 20

T
Tanous, Alex, 61, 62
Teed, Daniel, 50
telepathy, 30
Tower of London, 37
trains, 9, 13, 67, 70
Tulip Staircase, 72, 80

U
University of Virginia, 46
United States Department of Commerce, 36

V
Valley Forge, 67

W
wagons, 13
Walker, Mr. and Mrs., 17, 19
Wayne, General Anthony, 67
White House, 35